I LOVE YOU

Coupons

for MOM

For Mom—A.I.
For my Mom, Helen Blanken—L.M.

Text copyright © 2004 by Alison Inches. Illustrations copyright © 2004 by Laura Merer. All rights reserved.
Published by Price Stern Sloan, a division of Penguin Young Readers Group,
345 Hudson Street, New York, NY 10014. *PSS!* is a registered trademark of Penguin Group (USA) Inc.
Published simultaneously in Canada. Manufactured in China.

ISBN: 0-8431-0660-3

A B C D E F G H I J

I LOVE YOU Coupons for MOM

by Alison Inches

illustrated by Laura Merer

PSS!
PRICE STERN SLOAN

It's your special day! What can I do for you, Mom?
Would you like a clean car? Let me wash it!

To:

From:

Maybe you'd like to make cookies?
Let's make them together!

Perhaps you'd like to go to a concert? You've got it!

To:

From:

Coupon good for:

Hug Your Mom Song
(to the tune of "Row Your Boat")

Hug, hug, hug your mom
Hug and squeeze her tight.
Snuggly, wuggly, buggly, boo
A kiss and then good night!

You say you like fine art? Voilà!

BY ME

me ↓

Would you enjoy a fireside poetry reading? My pleasure!

Coupon good for:

One Poem

Selected by you or written by me. Here's one suggestion:

There's a neat little clock
In the school room it stands,
And it points to the time
With its two little hands.

And may we, like the clock,
Keep a face clean and bright,
With hands ever ready
To do what is right.

—Mother Goose

I know how much you like quiet time.
I can be as quiet as a mouse!

To:

From:

Coupon good for:

One Hour of Quiet Time

Things I can do during quiet time:
- Read a book • Write a letter
- Draw a picture • Write a story

Not one peep out of me!

To:

From:

You keep a beautiful house, Mom.
I can keep my room beautiful too!

Coupon good for:

Cleaning My Room

I can:

- Make my bed
- Put away my toys
- Empty my wastebasket
- Hang up my clothes
- Tidy my desk
- Organize my closet

Maybe you'd like help watering
the plants? Fill 'er up!

To:

From:

Coupon good for:

Watering the Plants

Indoor and outdoor plants included.

No expiration date!

To:

From:

How would you like some quality time together? Let's go!

Coupon good for:

One Walk

We can:
- Stop and smell the flowers
- Listen to the birds
- Count the animals
- Skip rocks

I can do all these things for your special day, but I bet I know what you want most. . .

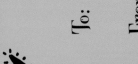

The very best me!

Coupon good for:

Cuddle time

Hugs and kisses included.

To:

From: